# Ruby Rogers
## Get a Life!

# Ruby Rogers
## Get a Life!

Sue Limb

Illustrations by Bernice Lum

BLOOMSBURY

## To Gladys Porter

First published in Great Britain in 2007 by Bloomsbury Publishing Plc
36 Soho Square, London, WID 3QY

A CIP catalogue record of this book is available from the British Library

ISBN 978 0 7475 8324 0

All papers used by Bloomsbury Publishing are natural, recyclable
products made from wood grown in well-managed forests.
The manufacturing processes conform to the environmental
regulations of the country of origin.

Printed in Great Britain by Clays Ltd, St Ives Plc

1 3 5 7 9 10 8 6 4 2

www.suelimbbooks.co.uk
www.bloomsbury.com

## CHAPTER 1
# I'll never forgive myself

A S I ARRIVED at the school gate I saw
Yasmin waiting for me over by the main door.
No way was I going to speak to her *ever again*. I
wouldn't even *look* at her. I wouldn't look at her
one more time in my *entire life*, even if we lived in
the same street. And if she dared to speak to me
today, I'd spit in her eye. I'd spit in *both* her eyes.

I pretended not to see her, went through the gate
and off across the yard, away from the doorway.
Through the crowd I saw Hannah picking her
nose in her usual charming dreamy way. Right! I'd

go and talk to her instead. When I was halfway there, I saw something out of the corner of my eye. Yasmin hurtling towards me.

'Ruby!' she shouted. 'Ruuuubeeeee!' I ignored her. 'RUUUUUBBBEEE!' she yelled. My eardrums almost shattered. I carried on walking towards Hannah, who was still picking her nose. If we ever have an Olympic nose-picking team, Hannah will be captain.

At this point somebody grabbed me. Yasmin. She threw her arms around me and hugged me, so, of course, I had to stop walking. I was still ignoring her, though. I just sort of grimly stared ahead. She grabbed my hand.

'Ruby!' pleaded Yasmin. 'Speak to me! Don't blank me like this! I'm soooo sorry! I was *soooo* wrong to say monkeys were stupid! I'll never forgive myself! I've got a present for you! Look! It's all wrapped up in green shiny paper!'

Something flashed and sparkled in the corner of my left eye. I wasn't going to look, though. I just went on staring in the other direction, at Hannah. (She still hadn't seen us, amazingly. She was totally unaware of our life-or-death struggle. She had started on the other nostril.)

'Ruby!' Yasmin's voice dropped to a hoarse whis-

per. 'You've got to be friends with me again. You've *got* to. I've had the weekend from *hell*. I couldn't sleep. I couldn't eat. You turned off your mobile. You told your mum to say you were out when I rang your landline. I've been punished enough!'

I went on staring into the distance. I hoped I was looking pale and grand. No way was I ever going to speak to Yasmin again – *ever*.

'My mum's made some of her grated cheese sandwiches,' Yasmin went on, whispering desperately now. 'You can have some.'

I hesitated. When I said I would never speak to Yasmin again, I had forgotten about the sandwiches. Her mum makes these absolutely incredible, amazing, heavenly sandwiches. She grates the cheese into tangy little piles and the bread is just wonderfully soft with crusty edges.

'How many?' I asked sternly.

'All! You can have them *all*!' shrieked Yasmin, mad with joy that I'd actually spoken to her. '*Please* say you forgive me. *Please* be friends again. I didn't mean it when I said your monkeys were stupid.'

'Why did you say it, then?' I turned to her for the first time and looked into her eyes. I hoped my eyes were glittering and cruel. But it was quite hard to keep up the cruel act when I saw that Yasmin had actually been crying. Her big black curly eyelashes were all wet, and there were wet streaks on her face.

'Why did you say monkeys were stupid?'

'I had a headache,' said Yasmin lamely. 'I felt bad.'

'When you attack monkeys,' I said solemnly, 'you attack me. OK?' I didn't want to drag this out too much, though. I was wondering how many sandwiches her mum had made, and whether we had time for one before the bell went for registration.

'I know, I know – I'll never say anything rude or horrid about monkeys ever again,' said Yasmin. 'Or any animals. Except possibly spiders. Here's your present. Are we friends again?'

She pushed the green shiny little parcel into my hands. I tried not to look interested. I tried to open it looking as if I just didn't care if I had a present or not. Inside was a small white box. I opened the box, and inside was a brooch – a brooch of a monkey! He had red eyes.

'He's got ruby eyes,' said Yasmin. 'Well, not real rubies. I don't think so anyway. But it's to show he's Ruby's. We got him at a car boot sale on Sunday. I used up two weeks' pocket money on him.'

I couldn't help smiling when I looked at him. He

had a cheeky grin and his ruby eyes flashed in the winter sunshine. I unfastened my coat and pinned him on my jumper.

'Thank you,' I said. 'He's very nice.' But I still tried to say it in a sort of grand voice, as if I was somebody important.

'Are we friends again, then?' asked Yasmin.

'OK,' I said, shrugging.

'Best friends?' said Yasmin. I nodded. She grabbed my hand. 'Oh thank *God!*' she whispered with a massive sigh. 'I promise I'll never say anything out of order, ever again.'

Just as I was about to make a polite enquiry about the cheese sandwiches, the bell rang. Typical!

'At break,' whispered Yasmin, as we walked into school, 'we'll go down on the field and have the sandwiches. OK?'

'I thought you said I could have all the sandwiches?'

'Oh, come on, Ruby!' Yasmin giggled. 'If you eat all the sandwiches, you'll get a tummy ache. Maybe even be sick! You can have more than me, though. And I'll tell you all about Holly's new boyfriend.'

'Holly's got a boyfriend?' This was terrible news. Holly's a gorgeous, glamorous teenage Goth and I was lining her up as girlfriend for my big brother, Joe. Especially now he'd split up from the tiresome Tiffany.

'I'll tell you all about it at break,' said Yasmin.

I was looking forward to break. Mainly the sandwiches, of course. But also the information. If Holly had a boyfriend I had to hatch a plot to split them up without Holly minding at all. Maybe I could make her boyfriend smell completely repulsive somehow. Perhaps I could make a kind of witches' brew of horrid-smelling stuff and squirt a bit on his jacket without him noticing.

I was so much looking forward to break. And I was glad Yasmin and I were friends again, to be honest. She'd cried, she'd apologised, she'd promised never to diss monkeys again, she'd bought me a present, she'd promised me most of her cheese sandwiches and she had all the gossip. As a candidate for best friend, I had to admit, right now she held all the aces.

We sat together at the back of the classroom. It was five-star accommodation. There was a radiator right next to us, and a spare chair for our bags. We settled down cosily and Yasmin reached under the table and during registration she squeezed my hand so hard, she almost broke several bones in my fingers. I grinned at her. The good old team was back together again. But then something unusual happened.

The door opened and the head teacher, Mrs Wakefield, walked in, together with a really weird-looking girl. She was pale and a bit spotty with dark circles under her eyes. She had wild silly hair and a big bottom and she kind of waddled.

'This is Lauren Potter,' said Mrs Wakefield. 'She's new to Ashcroft Primary and I know you're all going to make her very welcome indeed.'

Lauren blushed and looked at the floor. 'What a nerd!' whispered Yasmin. Our class teacher, Mrs Jenkins, shook hands with Lauren. Lauren shook hands kind of badly, as if she couldn't quite remember what hands were for.

'Welcome to Y10 Ashcroft, Lauren!' said Mrs Jenkins, smiling broadly and pretending, for a moment, not to be a werewolf. 'You're going to love it here. We're all mad, of course. Now, where will you sit? Ah yes, there's a chair at the back with Yasmin and Ruby.'

Disaster! Mrs J had dumped the nerd on us! Lauren made her way awkwardly towards us, tripping over people's bags and getting caught up in her own hair.

'Hannah, stop picking your nose!' said Mrs Jenkins. 'Now, Yasmin and Ruby, I know I can count on you to make Lauren feel at home. Yasmin and Ruby will look after you today, Lauren, but if there are any problems they can't sort out for you, you only have to ask me.'

Lauren finally arrived in our corner. Yasmin took our bags off the spare chair. Lauren tried to smile at us both at once and went sort of cross-eyed. She sat down. Close up, she had strange zombie eyes. Her coat smelt new. This was a total nightmare.

*Oh no*, I thought in despair. *Yasmin's going to have to offer her one of* my *cheese sandwiches!*

## CHAPTER 2
## You pig!

A T BREAK it was raining, so we all had to
stay indoors. Mrs Jenkins went off to the
staffroom for her cup of coffee and we sat on our
desks. There was a terrific noise, with everybody
talking and Froggo singing some stupid song from
his latest computer game.

'*Kill Kill Kill!*' he sang. '*Kill till you feel so
ill!*'

'Take no notice of Froggo,' I said, smiling at
Lauren. 'He's not really a cold-blooded killer. He's
really a pussycat.'

'Pardon?' said Lauren, blushing. 'Did you say something about a cat?' It *was* very noisy.

'That boy!' I shouted. 'He's quite nice really!' I pointed at Froggo. He pulled a face, making his eyes all bulgy. 'We call him Froggo!' I yelled.

'Poddo?' shouted Lauren above the din. This wasn't a great start to our relationship. Total failure to communicate.

I could communicate with Yasmin easily, though. She knew what I was thinking. I knew what she was thinking. We were both wishing Lauren could be beamed off to the Planet Tharg and leave us in peace.

'Is shish Thenkin spice?' asked Lauren.

'Wha?' I yelled.

'Is Mrs Jenkins nice?' shouted Lauren.

'No!' I cried. 'She's a werewolf!'

'What?' shouted Lauren.

'I'm going to the loo!' yelled Yasmin. 'I won't be long!'

And she pushed her way through the crowd. I watched her go with real pain. I knew she had those blinking cheese sandwiches in her bag and if this nerd Lauren hadn't been dumped on us, we could be eating them right now in a cosy corner somewhere.

'Have you got any brothers and sisters?' asked Lauren, moving in close and shouting in my ear.

'Yeah!' I yelled. 'One bro! Joe! He's sixteen and vile!'

'I've got two brothers and a sister!' yelled Lauren. 'They're all younger than me! Alfie and Roly and Alice!'

'Nice names!' I yelled back. I felt annoyed that Lauren had more brothers and sisters than me. It was almost as if she was showing off.

'Got any pets?' shouted Lauren.

'No!' I yelled back. 'Worse luck! My mum's a midwife and my dad's a geography teacher, so it wouldn't be fair to have a dog. We're out all day.'

There was a silence. I wondered what was keep-ing Yasmin. She's usually very quick on her visits to the loo.

'Have you got any pets?' I asked.

'Well, sort of,' said Lauren. 'Two sheepdogs, a pony and three cats.'

*What a show-off,* I thought. *I'm going to hate her forever.*

'Plus the farm animals,' Lauren went on.

'You live on a farm?' I asked. Lauren suddenly seemed slightly different. 'What animals have you got?'

'Oh, about two hundred cattle,' said Lauren. 'About nine hundred sheep. The lambs are just being born now. And free-range hens. And we've just got two pigs and they've both had piglets.'

'Piglets!' I shrieked, possibly in a piglet-like way. 'How many?'

'Fifteen,' said Lauren. 'You can come and see them one day, if you like.'

'Yeah,' I said, trying not to sound too keen. 'Great.'

My mind was wandering, to tell you the truth. I was having hunger pangs. Where was Yasmin with those divine cheese sandwiches? How could she be so mean as to leave me stranded with Lauren like this?

I didn't even mind donating one of my sandwiches to Lauren. Just so long as *I* could have one. My tummy was rumbling now like a thunderstorm in the Rockies. Luckily there was so much noise in the classroom that nobody heard.

'Do you want to go to the loo?' I asked.

'No,' said Lauren. 'I'm all right. I hardly ever go.'

Once again it seemed to me that she was trying to score points. OK, she had more animals than Noah in his ark, and a family the size of a football team, but did she really need to boast about how she never had to use the loo?

'I hardly ever go, either,' I said coolly, even though I was starting to want to go right now, and the more I thought about it, the worse it got.

I was beginning to feel quite bad. I was faint with hunger and dying for the loo. But just then the bell went, and any minute now Mrs Jenkins would come marching back in.

Yasmin appeared and sat down in the chair next to the radiator. I noticed crumbs around her mouth. I slid down into the chair next to her. Lauren also sat down.

'Have you been eating the sandwiches?' I whispered in Yasmin's ear. 'Give me one quick! I'm starving! I've just got time before Jenko gets back!'

'I'm sorry, Ruby!' whispered Yasmin, 'but there aren't any left. I met Hannah in the corridor and I was eating one, so I had to offer her one. And then Emma Goodheart turned up and demanded one too.'

'You pig!' I hissed. 'Those sandwiches were mine. You said so yourself.'

'You can have all of them tomorrow,' said Yasmin, licking her lips and wiping her mouth on her sleeve. 'They weren't very nice anyway. The bread was stale.'

I knew she was lying. Her mum's bread is never stale. I started to hate her again. It had been a mistake, allowing her to get round me with her promises of cheese sandwiches. I nearly hated

Lauren because of her boasting, but I almost hated Yasmin worse.

'Right!' said Mrs Jenkins, marching into the class and banging her bag down on the desk. 'Now I hope nobody's forgotten what a special day it is on Friday?'

'No, miss! St Valentine's!' yelled Sophie Grant. Froggo made the sound of somebody being sick.

'Quiet, Dan!' Mrs Jenkins snapped at him. 'Now don't forget the party. Oh – Lauren – we're having a fancy-dress party after school on Friday. It's to raise enough money to buy some goats for poor families in Africa. The fancy-dress theme is animals. OK?'

Lauren nodded. I was surprised she didn't take the chance of boasting about her huge menagerie.

'Right,' said Mrs Jenkins, 'don't forget to bring your costumes with you on Friday. You can change into them after last lesson. There's a letter here for your parents, to remind them of the details.' She gave out the letters.

'You'll be coming as a monkey, won't you, Ruby?' said Yasmin.

'No need for any special costume, then!' said Froggo. Everybody laughed. I tried to smile as if I didn't mind being the laughing stock of the whole class. I was really cross with Yasmin and Froggo for teasing me like that. Especially as I was so hungry. Yasmin had given Hannah and Emma Goodheart my cheese sandwiches! OK, I was hungry and humiliated. But I would have my revenge.

## CHAPTER 3
# What's going on?

AT LUNCHTIME things went from bad to worse. It was still raining, so we all had to stay in again. As we were queueing for our lunch, Yasmin pushed ahead a bit in the queue and started to talk to Hannah about something. She was trying to look as if they were talking about something important, but I knew she was just trying to get away from Lauren. Something important? Hah! She was probably asking what was Hannah's bogey score for the morning.

Lauren stood beside me, looking miserable. I just

had to talk to her, even though I hadn't a clue what to say.

'Do you like pizza?' I asked. She wrinkled her nose and shook her head. 'What about jacket potatoes?' I said. Lauren shook her head. 'Hamburgers?' It was a no. 'Chicken?' Another no. 'Curry?' Lauren shook her head and pulled a very disgusted face.

'Well, what in the world do you like, then?' I exploded. Maybe she was from another planet where they ate only paper.

'I like cheese sandwiches,' she said in a very quiet, apologetic voice. 'And chips.'

*What a horrid coincidence*, I thought. This was bad news. Yasmin was going to have to share her cheese sandwiches between three from now on. Although knowing Yasmin, she would find a sneaky way to avoid it. Even now she was sneaking and snaking her way up through the queue, further and further away from me.

She turned and looked at me, and beckoned. There was a playful but irritated look on her face, as if I was being a dull old nerd, talking to Lauren instead of excitingly queue-jumping with her. I gave her a dirty look and turned back to Lauren.

'What about ice cream?' I said. Everybody likes ice cream, for goodness' sake. If Lauren said she didn't like ice cream, it would be proof she was an alien. She nodded, and a hint of a smile crossed her face.

'Specially chocolate!' she said.

'Lauren!' said Froggo, who was behind us in the queue. 'Are you foreign?' It rhymed. Froggo grinned. Usually I find him hilarious, but today he just seemed silly.

'No,' said Lauren, looking rather frightened.

'Lauren,' said Froggo again, leaning in close and goggling his eyes at her, 'Forgive my asking, but are you Harry Potter's sister?'

Everybody laughed. Except Lauren. I could see she was totally fed up with jokes like this. Her eyes filled with tears. She turned away and ignored him.

I felt a sudden surge of temper. Today had been vile so far. Yasmin had pretended to make it up with me, but where was she now? Already choosing her pizza and salad up ahead, chatting to Hannah, while I struggled to look after this shy lumpy Lauren, who wouldn't stick up for herself or say a word louder than a whisper. And now stupid Froggo was going to make her cry.

Something exploded inside me. I wheeled round and gave Froggo the most almighty kick on the

shin. His eyes went enormous for a split second, he opened his mouth and a huge shout came out: 'AAAAAAAAOOOOOOOOWWWWW!'

Mrs Briggs the dinner lady marched down the queue and glared at him. Froggo was hopping about, rubbing his leg.

'What's going on?' snapped Mrs Briggs. She's quite old with grey hair and thick frightening glasses that make her eyes look huge.

'Ruby kicked me!' wailed Froggo. Mrs Briggs glared at me. Her eyes were bigger than saucers. More like dinner plates.

'Is this true, Ruby?' she asked.

'I only kicked him because he was being horrible to Lauren,' I said. 'She's new.'

Mrs Briggs looked suspicious.

'Go to the back of the queue!' she said. 'All three of you! I'm not having any of this!'

We trailed off miserably to the back of the queue. Froggo wasn't speaking to me because I'd kicked him. I wasn't speaking to Lauren because I'd run out of things to say. And Lauren wasn't speaking because she was new and felt so miserable, she wished she'd never been born. To be honest, I was beginning to wish she'd never been born, too.

When we finally reached the food counter there was nothing much left except tuna mayonnaise salad. I had to have some even though I knew it would make me feel faintly sick all afternoon. Froggo had the remains of the chilli con carne, which had gone dried up and cold, and Lauren had a bread roll. Froggo went off and sat at the furthest corner, away from me and Lauren.

I had now lost all the friends I'd ever had: Yasmin had finished her lunch and gone off with Hannah. I was beginning to feel terrible about kicking Froggo. His poor leg! What had made me lose it like that?

The rest of the afternoon passed in a horrid blur.

Yasmin sat on one side of me, Lauren on the other. We were supposed to be painting our favourite animal. I tried to paint a monkey, of course, but it turned out a bit too human.

'Is that a self-portrait, Ruby?' giggled Yasmin. She hadn't even noticed that I wasn't speaking to her. She can be so insensitive.

Yasmin had painted a bird with fabulous long tail feathers, all pink and gold. Lauren had painted something very odd: brown and tapering at both ends.

'It looks like a piece of poo!' whispered Yasmin in hysterics. I nearly laughed, but I remembered just in time that I was supposed to be blanking Yasmin, so I saved it up to laugh about later.

'What animal is that, Lauren?' I asked.

'It's a pangolin,' she said in a very quiet voice.

'A *what*?'

'A pangolin. It's a scaly anteater,' said Lauren, looking embarrassed.

'What a show-off!' whispered Yasmin in my ear. I wished she wouldn't do that. It was so obvious she was saying something about Lauren. Lauren looked hurt and turned back to her poo-like favourite beast. She gave it cute little claw-like feet.

'It rolls itself up into a ball when it's frightened,' she said, looking sadly at me with her big shadowy eyes. I realised, in a flash, that Lauren wanted to *be* a pangolin, and I could hardly blame her.

Could the day get any worse? Eventually the bell rang. It was home time. Yasmin rushed off to tell her mum she'd been invited to have tea at Hannah's and, of course, I found myself with Lauren. We put our coats on in silence. My mind was a complete blank. Looking after Lauren was like dragging a bag of sand about. It was going to be like this tomorrow and the day after. Maybe for ever.

We walked out to the gate, and a small thin woman wearing a sheepskin-type jacket waved.

'That's my mum,' said Lauren. I wondered how such a small mum could produce such a big nerdy daughter. 'Mum, this is Ruby,' said Lauren.

'Hello, Ruby! How nice to meet you!' said Lauren's mum, smiling. 'Can we give you a lift home or anything?'

'No, thanks,' I said. 'I'm fine.' I had had enough of Lauren for one day.

'Thanks for looking after me today, Ruby,' said Lauren. 'It was really really nice of you.' And she smiled. *Smiled*.

'Oh, no, it was nothing,' I shrugged, and backed off. I felt myself blushing. I was ashamed of all the rude and nasty things I'd thought about poor Lauren. I sort of waved awkwardly, and we parted.

I began to trudge home. Could life get any worse? At least it had stopped raining. But I *so* wished I was some kind of animal rather than Ruby Rogers. I would have given anything to be a snow leopard, or an elephant, or anything that didn't have to go to school.

'Hi, Ruby!' called a cheery voice. I looked up.

Could life get any worse? It certainly could. There, beaming at me, was Holly Helvellyn, my Gothic role model, actually *holding hands with a boy.* Disaster! And he was the weirdest-looking boy I had ever seen in my life.

CHAPTER 4

# I hope that's not an omen . . .

RUBY, THIS is Dom,' said Holly. 'Dom, this is Ruby. Joe Rogers' little sister.'

Dom looked down at me with faint disgust. He was extremely tall, with a pale haughty face and black hair down to his shoulders. He had an earring and a nose-ring.

'Dom plays in a band,' said Holly, looking impressed. 'It's called BioHazard.'

I didn't care if his band had been on TV or played at Glastonbury: if he couldn't be bothered to smile at me, or even nod, I couldn't be bothered with him either. I hated him for being there and spoiling things between me and Holly. If he hadn't been there, she'd have walked home with me and talked about my monkeys and maybe even come in for a cup of coffee or something.

And she might have got talking to Joe, and because Joe had been ditched by the horrible Tiffany, they might have managed to set up a date at long last, and then Holly would be round my house all the time instead of Tiffany. I hated it when Tiffany had tea with us. She never said 'Thank you' properly to my mum, and she'd always have the last sandwich and say, 'Yeah, why not?' instead of 'Oh, thank you! How lovely . . . Well, if nobody else wants it . . . ?'

Basically she was a greedy cow, and she never bothered to talk to me, and sometimes she even talked in some kind of elaborate code to Joe when I was there, like: 'Shall we go and buy some you-know-what and go and do stuff over at what's-his-name's?' As if I cared what stupid things they were planning!

Whereas Holly was always totally nice to me. She designed and planned my secret surprise tree house, she turned me into a tiger with her face paints, she lent me her fancy-dress bird costume for Hallowe'en, and when Yasmin and I had had our biggest row ever, she got us together and forced us to make friends again.

'How're things with Yasmin these days?' asked Holly. 'Yasmin's Zerrin's little sister – you know, Zerrin Saffet, with the long black hair,' she said to Dom. Dom frowned slightly, as if he was very bored by all Holly's friends and wished she would shut up about them.

'Oh, fine,' I said. 'I'm just never going to speak to her again for about three days, I should think.'

Holly laughed, and looked at Dom as if to say *Isn't my young friend a witty little devil?* But

Dom just went on frowning and staring into space as if he was planning to poison some pussycats, or possibly grow a beard like black barbed wire.

'You're kidding, right?' Holly asked me.

'No,' I said. 'There was this new girl at school, and she was dead boring, and we were supposed to be looking after her, and Yasmin went off with Hannah and left me with Lauren, who, like, hardly ever talks ever.'

'Oh no!' said Holly and laughed merrily as if this was the most amusing thing since last night's *Simpsons*. She had stopped really caring about me. I could tell. The old Holly would have taken me seriously. Now my problems were just a joke.

'Tell Yasmin from me she's got to stop messing you about or I'll turn her into a toad!' said Holly with a sideways grin at Dom. 'And don't worry, Rube, it'll sort itself out! You guys are a legend when it comes to rows!'

'Yeah,' I said with a sigh.

'We've gotta go now!' said Holly. 'We're going to the Dolphin Cafe for some kind of boring Mad Hatter's Tea Party with the rest of Dom's band!' She looked thrilled. As if nothing could be more exciting than a glamorous get-together with dumb Dom and his zombie friends. Especially not the problems of Ruby Rogers, her former friend and protégé.

I waved goodbye and trailed off home. Holly waved with a peculiar sparkly kind of flash of the eyes, but she was papering over the cracks and we both knew it. I was yesterday's girl. Dom was now the king of the castle in Holly's eyes. He grandly ignored me as they walked off towards the Dolphin Cafe.

I tried to make the journey home more interesting by not treading on any cracks in the pavement, but to be honest it was total Dullsville being on my own, instead of enjoying the company of the fascinating Holly. Eventually I arrived home and

wished we had a dog. A dog would have welcomed me with frantic tail-wagging and that laughing thing dogs do. But, of course, we don't have one.

Mum was in the kitchen, peeling some onions and crying. It was only the onions, obviously, irritating her eyes, but it sort of suited my mood.

'Blast these blinking onions!' said Mum. That counts as swearing if you're a Welsh midwife. 'Don't just dump your bag there, Ruby!' she yelled. 'Take it up to your room and do your homework now, before supper!'

As I passed the sitting room I heard music. I glanced in through the open door and saw a truly dreadful sight. There was Joe, sitting on the sofa, and Tiffany was next to him! Wrapped round him like a boa constrictor! Tiffany was back!

'Hi, Ruby!' she called. 'How are you doin'?'

I had to stop and be polite to her. I don't know which was worse: Holly not wanting to talk to me, or Tiffany wanting to talk to me. I knew her game. She was trying to get all Joe's family on her side. I had seen Joe with tears in his eyes when she had dumped him. He didn't know I'd seen him crying, but I had. I hated her for dumping him, and now I hated her even more for slinking and smarming her way back on to our sofa.

'Fine thanks,' I said. I stood out in the hall and just looked in through the door, in what I hoped was a distant and unfriendly way.

'Come in properly and talk to me!' said Tiffany. 'I haven't seen you for ages.'

'I've got to go upstairs and do my homework,' I said. 'Mum's just told me.'

'Oh, right,' said Tiffany. She was secretly relieved she had an excuse not to talk to me all that much. 'Just tell me – how's everything? What are you and what's-her-name up to? Your friend? With the funny name?'

'Yasmin,' I said. 'She's fine.'

'OK,' said Joe, who had been searching through

the DVDs. 'This or this?' He held up two DVDs for Tiffany to choose from. I made my escape upstairs.

At least my bedroom was still marvellous. Not many people have a tree house indoors to sleep in. My monkeys looked down at me from the sleeping platform.

'Guys,' I informed them, 'I've had the day from hell. Frankly, at the moment, life sucks.'

'Sorry to hear that,' said Stinker, the fat boss monkey, 'but who's that on your sweatshirt?'

'Another monkey!' said Funky.

'Does he play tennis?' asked Hewitt – he is total-

ly sport-mad and never talks about anything else.

I had forgotten about my new monkey brooch that Yasmin had given me. I looked down at it. It was cute, I had to admit. Its red eyes twinkled. Apparently Yasmin had spent two weeks' pocket money on it.

'What's his name?' said Funky. 'Or is it a girl?'

'Yeah,' I said. 'It's a girl monkey called – uh – Priscilla, maybe.'

I unfastened the brooch monkey to introduce her properly to the other monkeys, but somehow I messed it up and pricked my finger. It bled. I sucked it, annoyed.

'Hmmm,' said Stinker. 'I hope that's not an omen . . .'

Yep. I could always count on Stinker to cheer me up.

## CHAPTER 5

# Wow! It was a masterpiece!

'OK GUYS,' I said. 'Can I have silence, please? I have to do some homework.'

I had to read a chapter of a book about the lives of girls and boys two hundred years ago. I opened the book and found chapter seven.

Suddenly Mum burst into my room, carrying some ironed shirts. She put them in my drawer.

'Ruby!' she whispered, looking frazzled, 'Supper's in half an hour, and don't ask for seconds because Tiffany's staying so it's visitors first.' Mum looked a bit fed up that Tiffany was staying.

When Tiffany was going out with Joe before, I overheard Mum say to Dad, 'I sometimes wonder if she actually does have a home of her own!' Hmm. Back to history.

*The lives of most children in the nineteenth century were hard and cruel,* the book said. *Many never went to school at all.* Hard and cruel? Not having to go to school? It sounded like paradise to me.

*Some started work as young as six, and laboured from dawn till nightfall in crowded, noisy, dangerous factories.* Well, school can be crowded, noisy and dangerous – you could get kicked, for example. Suddenly I remembered that I'd kicked Froggo just for asking Lauren if she was Harry Potter's sister. If only I could turn the clock back, I would never have committed that foul. A simple elbow in the ribs would have been quite sufficient.

I decided to make it up to Froggo tomorrow by offering him some kind of delicious treat. I would have to steal something from the food cupboard. He loves biscuits. A couple of custard creams should do the trick.

I now had to write the diary of a Victorian chimney sweep, describing how he had to climb up inside the chimneys. I chose my blackest pen.

*My name is Alfie Bisto,* I wrote. *I am ten yeares*

*olde and I werk as a chimbley sweap.* I assumed Alfie would not be very good at spelling. In fact, if most Victorian children never went to school, how would Alfie have managed to write a diary at all? Eh? Eh? Explain that, Miss Jenkins, you fearsome beast, if you would . . .

*Today I climed three chimnbleys in a big howse in London towne,* I wrote in strange loopy old-fashioned writing. *In one I founde a jackdawe's nest and ye birdes floo down and pecked at my haire. All ye soot fell into my eyese and ye duste made me coff.*

I had almost moved myself to tears by the horrible life of Alfie. I was beginning to get quite fond of him.

*When I came downe ye chimnbley,* I wrote, making my writing even more ragged and stressy, *my unkinde master kicked me becos I was slowe and I coffed soote all over the lady's chaire.*

Wow! It was a masterpiece! I thought it would be fun to kind of dirty it up and put sooty fingerprints all over it. I got out my paintbox and mixed up some black and grey. Then I loaded up my paintbrush and flicked a scatter of black dots all over the paper. It looked great.

Next I dabbled my fingers in the paint and decorated the margins of the page with grubby

thumb prints. Poor Alfie! I wondered if the children who had to climb chimneys ever had a bath. I had a funny kind of feeling that in the olden days, most people didn't even have bathrooms.

*Now I must finishe my dairey,* I wrote, my dirty hands making it even more realistic. *I have onlie had a crust of bred for my super. I am going to slepe on a sack under my master's kichen table. I hop the dog Bert will not bight me.*

Well! If I didn't get an A for this, there was no justice. I went to the bathroom and washed my hands. Then Mum called upstairs that supper was ready.

43

## CHAPTER 6
# Dad tried not to look gutted

'DID YOU FINISH your homework?'
Mum asked, ladling out the lasagne.

'Yes,' I told her. I could see that the lasagne wasn't really designed for five people. It was quite small. We were all going to get less because of blinking Tiffany. She and Joe were sitting at the other end of the table. She was playing with the back of his hair and telling him he should grow a ponytail. I hate the way she's all over him like a rash.

I ate my small portion of lasagne in silence. Mum

and Dad were arguing about whether or not to get a steam cleaner.

'Is there any pudding?' I asked, as I finished the lasagne.

'Fruit or a yogurt,' said Mum, looking vaguely annoyed. 'Wait till everyone's finished, though, Ruby.'

I hated all this polite stuff. Tiffany takes ages over her food, partly because she's always stopping to curl her hair back behind her ears or play silly little games with Joe.

Mum got out the yogurts. There were four of them. We all stared at them and did a bit of mental arithmetic. Somebody was going to have to go without.

'Tiffany,' said Mum, with a bright smile that wasn't quite the real thing, 'would you like a yogurt?'

'Oooh, yes please!' said Tiffany. The greedy cow.

'Which one?' asked Mum.

'The toffee one,' said Tiffany. She didn't even say *please*. Honestly! Mum separated the yogs and handed the toffee one to Tiffany. Dad tried not to look gutted. The toffee one is his favourite.

'Ruby?' said Mum.

I *so* wanted a yogurt – especially the blackcurrant one, which was my favourite. But I felt so cross about Tiffany bagging Dad's yogurt, that I didn't want to be greedy like her. I shook my head.

'No?' said Mum, sounding really surprised.

'Had enough,' I said. I was talking about Tiffany, too. Secretly. I'd certainly had enough of her. A pity Joe didn't feel the same.

'Dad? Joe?' Mum offered the remaining three yogs around. Now I'd heroically refrained from having a yogurt, there were enough for everybody. I could almost feel angelic wings sprouting from my back.

Joe grabbed the raspberry yogurt, Mum had the pineapple one, but Dad kind of sighed and shook his head.

'No,' he said. 'I'm trying to re-educate my taste-buds.'

'Hey!' said Tiffany, with a horrible yogurty grin, 'That's funny! Cos you're like, a teacher, yeah?'

Mum laughed politely. Dad smiled. Joe ignored her. I watched the remaining yogurt, sitting unclaimed on the table. Blackcurrant. My favourite. I wasn't going to have it now, but later, when everybody else was busy, I'd tiptoe to the fridge and secretly gobble it up. My mouth was already watering at the thought. It was fine being saintly, but I wasn't sure it was quite enough fun.

'I hope my tastebuds are more receptive to my teaching style than 4G were today,' said Dad, politely trying to make something of Tiffany's silly joke.

There was a brief silence. People eating yogurts finished and put down their spoons.

'Would you like to clear up that last yogurt for me, Tiffany?' asked Mum. She was only being polite. *No, no, Mum!* I thought in horror. Tiffany's greedy eyes lit up. She stared at my yogurt.

'Well, OK, then,' she said. 'Just to, like, clear it up.' And she reached out her paw and grabbed it. No please or thank you, again, of course. She has absolutely zero manners.

I felt physical pain as I watched her eat my yogurt. I glared. She was so obsessed with filling her face, she didn't notice. But Mum did.

'Ruby!' she said sharply, to get my attention. 'What happened in school today?'

I didn't want to start on the Lauren saga, because that was a bit too personal. I didn't want to let Tiffany know all about my feelings.

'Oh, we were talking about the fancy-dress party on St Valentine's Day,' I said. 'We've got to go as animals.'

'Ooh! Lovely!' said Tiffany. 'What are you going to go as? Oh, wait, silly me − a monkey, of course!'

'No need for fancy dress at all, then,' said Joe. I ignored him.

'Joe!' said Mum. 'Don't be silly. So, Ruby − fancy dress, that's nice, love. But you'd better get a move on organising your costume if the party's on Friday. You could ask Holly to help you make a costume, couldn't you? She helped you with that lovely Hallowe'en outfit, didn't she?'

'I think Holly's too busy,' I said. I knew she wouldn't want to come over to our house now Joe was back with Tiffany.

'Holly's going out with Dom Kendall,' said Tiffany, glancing at Joe to see if there was any reaction. 'He plays in a band called BioHazard.'

'God help him, then,' said Dad. 'I wasted the best years of my youth in Mother Gumption's Bunch of Feathers.'

'Was that your band?' asked Tiffany. 'What a weird name!'

'We were pathetic old hippies,' said Dad. 'It was cool to be punks when I was young. But we wanted to be different.'

'I'm going to be different, too,' I said, proud of Dad and wanting Tiffany to shut up.

'You already are different!' laughed Tiffany. 'You're the most different little girl I've ever met!'

And she laughed in a way that was far from pleasant. I gave her a venomous look. 'You want to be a gangster, and you've got a tree house in your bedroom!' Tiffany went on. 'And you don't like dolls – you prefer monkeys!'

I could feel my vest melting as I tried to refrain from murdering her right there at the table.

'We're all different, aren't we, really?' said Mum, trying to smooth things over. 'Apart from twins, of course.'

'I wish I had a twin,' sighed Tiffany. 'That would be so cool!' The thought of two Tiffanys was, for a second, so frightful that I had to close my eyes in order to avoid being sick.

'So what animal are you going as, Rube?' asked Dad.

'I don't know yet,' I said.

'Why don't you ask Holly if you can borrow that bird costume again?' suggested Mum. 'That wouldn't be any trouble.'

'I don't want to wear something I've worn before!' I snapped. 'That would be lame!'

'I'll help you make a costume, Rube!' gushed Tiffany. My heart sank. 'We'll have loads of laughs! You don't have to be a boring old monkey! Maybe you could be a snake! Or a spider! Or a giraffe!'

I was so furious, I couldn't speak. First, she had called me Rube, without being given permission. Then she had said 'boring old monkey' – reason enough for me never to speak to her again! I made a secret vow to pee in her handbag at the first opportunity.

Lastly, she had suggested such a stupid, impossible list of animals. How could I go as a snake, for goodness' sake? My arms and legs would have to be in a kind of tube. I wouldn't be able to move.

How could I go as a spider? I'd have to have six false legs, and they would get in the way and knock everything over. And all my friends would scream and run away when they saw me. Yasmin has a major spider phobia.

As for a giraffe – don't make me laugh. Where would my face be? Looking out of the giraffe's chest, presumably. And the first time I walked through a doorway, the giraffe would break its neck. Tiffany was an idiot.

'Thanks, but I've arranged to make my costume with Yasmin,' I said coldly.

'I can help you both!' beamed Tiffany. 'Tell her to come round tomorrow afternoon, and we'll make a start on it.'

How could she keep going on and on when I'd already said we didn't need her ham-fisted help? I just kind of shrugged.

'Say thank you to Tiffany for being so kind as to help you, Ruby!' said Mum sharply.

'Thanks,' I said, and shrugged again, as if to suggest an extra message along the lines of *EAT MY SHORTS.*

I noticed Mum didn't tell Tiffany to say thank you after devouring almost the whole stockpile of family yogurts. Life was so unfair.

'We'll have an amazing time,' said Tiffany, grinning at me with blackcurrant yogurt – *my* blackcurrant yogurt – all over her teeth. 'You could go as an elephant, and Yasmin could go as a dolphin.' Then she burped.

I could hardly wait.

BURP!

## CHAPTER 7
# I so am stressed out!

I HURRIED INTO the schoolyard next morning, desperate to tell Yasmin all about horrendous Tiffany. But there was no sign of her. I immediately caught sight of Lauren, standing alone over by the wall. Instantly I looked away, as if I was desperate to find somebody. Of course, I was. Anybody but Lauren.

Where was Froggo? I had to apologise to him for kicking him. Where was Yasmin? I had to tell her all my troubles and receive sympathy and support. As I scanned the playground, somehow, by accident, I looked back in Lauren's direction and our eyes met. Her face lit up in a desperate needy smile. I couldn't help feeling sorry for her. I smiled back.

She took a step towards me, then hesitated. I could tell she was wanting to come over and talk, but she didn't want to be a nuisance. It would have been really mean to turn away after the smile. And I couldn't see Yasmin or Froggo anywhere, so I thought I might as well go over.

'Hi, Ruby!' said Lauren. 'How are you? You look a bit – uh, stressed out.'

'I so am stressed out!' I said. 'My bro has got this evil girlfriend called Tiffany. – Wait! Promise me you don't know her.'

'I don't know anybody called Tiffany,' said Lauren. 'Is she horrible?'

'She's worse than horrible,' I assured her. 'Last night, right? We were having our supper, and Mum had bought one of those little four-packs of yogurts, because there are four of us. But Tiffany gate-crashed our supper and had, like, two yogurts. Two! One was my dad's favourite and one was mine.'

'How horrible!' said Lauren. 'I hope your brother dumps her. Have a piece of chocolate.' She took a small chocolate bar out of her pocket and broke it in half. She offered me one half. I was surprised, and, of course, pleased. But I hesitated.

'Thanks,' I said, 'but I can't have all that! Break a little bit off.'

'Have it!' insisted Lauren, pushing the half into my hand. 'It'll cheer you up.'

'Thanks very much,' I said. The smell of chocolate was wonderful. The taste was amazing. 'You're a star!' I said chocolatishly. Lauren smiled. It was a small, nervous sort of smile, but it was real.

Suddenly Yasmin and Hannah appeared, laughing and pulling each other's coats. Hannah was

running in front of Yasmin, and Yas was holding on to Hannah's back. They sort of cannoned into us, and I nearly dropped my last bit of chocolate.

'Hi, Rube!' screeched Yasmin. 'Guess what! Hannah and I are going to the fancy-dress party as a pantomime horse!'

'My mum's making us the costume!' said Hannah. 'She's nearly finished it already! It's going to be amazing!'

My blood ran cold. I needed Yasmin to make her costume with me, so I could escape from horrible Tiffany.

'What are you going as, Lauren?' I asked. I was so furious with Yasmin, I couldn't even speak to her. She was supposed to be my best friend! If she was going to be a pantomime horse with anybody, it should be me.

'Er . . .' said Lauren. 'I'm not sure. I think maybe a lion. Mum says we could make a mane out of orange wool.'

Lauren, a lion? A mouse would have been more appropriate. It wasn't funny, though. Nothing was funny at the moment, what with Yasmin and Hannah horsing around and ignoring me.

'What are you going as, Ruby?' asked Lauren.

'A hippo!' yelled Yasmin. 'She's got the figure for

it!' Everybody knew this was a joke, because I am *so* not fat. It wasn't even remotely funny, though.

'Which end of the horse are you going to be?' I asked Yasmin in a sarcastic voice. 'The back end, presumably?'

Just then the bell rang, saving us from any more nastiness. I felt really angry with Yasmin as we lined up in our class groups. I was almost angrier with her than I had been the night before with Tiffany.

OK, Tiffany had been horrid but she wasn't supposed to be my best friend or anything. Yasmin was just acting weird at the moment, and I knew

it was because she didn't want to have to bother with Lauren. When she and Hannah had run up to us just now in the yard, she hadn't even said hello to Lauren – even though yesterday Mrs Jenkins had asked both of us to look after Lauren. Not just me.

And right now, Yasmin had gone ahead of me in the line. She was standing next to Hannah. I was towards the back, with Lauren.

As we filed into the classroom I made a strange, slightly weird but comforting decision. I really, really *was* going to get my revenge on Yasmin, somehow. But what was the revenge going to be? I wasn't sure yet.

After registration and assembly and stuff, we settled down in our classroom. Mrs Jenkins collected the homework. I had enjoyed writing the diary of the chimney sweep boy. As Mrs Jenkins walked around the room collecting the work, Yasmin was whispering to Hannah. They both giggled. I wasn't invited to share this delightful little joke.

Mrs Jenkins arrived at our table. She collected the work from Yasmin, Hannah and Lauren. Then she came to me. I handed it to her.

'This is a bit messy, Ruby!' she said, looking cross.

'Please, miss, it's because he's a chimney sweep,' I

said. 'I thought he would have sooty hands and stuff.' Mrs Jenkins's face changed. She looked at the work again, then down at me.

'I see,' she said. 'As usual, Ruby, you've gone a bit too far. But I can see what you're driving at.'

After she'd collected all the work, Mrs Jenkins asked us to write down a list of all the animals who came out at night.

'Owls,' I wrote. I wondered if I could have revenge on Yasmin by hiding a live owl in her wardrobe. It could poo on all her clothes and frighten her to death by flying out right in her face when she opened the door.

It was a great idea, but kind of difficult to organise. Where was I going to get a live owl? How was I going to smuggle it into her house? Under my jumper? What if it hooted and flapped and gave the game away?

What other animals come out at night? Lauren was writing away quite fast. I peeped at her work. *Toad*, she'd written. I didn't want to copy her, but I wondered for a minute if I might be able to take revenge on Yasmin with a toad. A toad in her schoolbag? A toad in her PE kit? A toad on her pillow when she woke up, first thing in the morning? A toad on her breakfast plate?

*Bats*, I wrote. A bat would be ideal. If only I could organise it so a bat flew into Yasmin's hair. That would make her scream! Brilliant, brilliant, brilliant! But how was I going to lay my hands on a bat? I got the feeling they might all be hibernating, anyway, at this time of year.

Yasmin pushed me a little note. Making sure Mrs Jenkins wasn't looking, I unfolded it. *Another animal that comes out at night*, it said. *The Slow Lauren.*

I crumpled up the paper and put it in my pocket. I ignored Yasmin. How could she be so mean? Lauren was sitting right next to me and could easily have seen it.

I know there is an animal called a slow loris, so I suppose that was part of the joke as well. I am very interested in animals, but I don't think you should call people names like that.

I chewed the end of my pen and stared out of the window. Considering how much I loved animals, I wasn't looking forward to this St Valentine's Day animal fancy-dress party one little bit.

It was going to be bad enough, anyway, with Tiffany slobbering all over Joe in a valentiney way and sending him cards and stuff. Wait! That was it! *St Valentine's*! That was how I'd take revenge on Yasmin! Brilliant! Perfect! I'd just had the best idea since ideas were invented.

## CHAPTER 8
# I could hardly wait

YASMIN WAS fairly horrid for the rest of the day. She shared her cheese sandwiches with Hannah at break, and sat with her at lunch. Lauren stuck close to me all the time, rabbiting on about stuff. Half the time I didn't listen, because I was planning my revenge so carefully.

I had been hoping to apologise to Froggo for kicking him, but he was away. I hoped he wasn't ill because of the kick. I had a brief nightmare in which a police car came round to our house and arrested me.

'I hope Froggo isn't away because of my kick,' I said, half to myself, half to Lauren, as we put our coats on at the end of the day.

'It was nice of you to stick up for me, Ruby,' said Lauren in her quiet, woolly voice, 'but really, there was no need. People make jokes about Harry Potter all the time. I'm used to it.'

When we got outside we saw Yasmin going off with Hannah and her mum. She looked back at me, waved madly and grinned as if nothing was wrong. Then she made a horse-riding sort of mime so I'd know they were going off to Hannah's to try out the pantomime horse.

As I waited for my mum to come and pick me up, I thought bitterly what fun it would be for them to be in a pantomime horse together. Plus Hannah's mum is a designer and the horse was going to be fabulous. Hannah's mum has a full-length chocolate brown sheepskin coat and it's all soft and expensive-looking, not like my mum's old stiff'n'smelly sheepskin coat she got from the charity shop.

'Would you like to come back for tea at my house, Ruby?' murmured Lauren in her soft squashy voice. I tried not to look alarmed.

'Oh, thanks,' I said. 'Maybe another time? Because my mum's coming today and I've got to go and do some stuff with her.'

'OK,' said Lauren. Her mum's car had just arrived. I felt mean saying no to her.

'I'd love to come another time,' I added. I didn't want to hurt her feelings, even though I really didn't want to go to tea at her house much at all. Lauren was OK, but she was kind of dull. I really missed Yasmin's naughty streak.

However, Yasmin's naughty streak had definitely got out of control this time. She was so irresponsible. She'd just basically waltzed off for two days in a row, now, leaving me alone with Lauren. I had to have my revenge, and as soon as I got home I was going to make a start.

'Got any homework today, Ruby?' asked Mum.

'Yes,' I told her. 'I've got a bit.' I didn't want to make it sound too interesting. I didn't want her coming up to my room and breathing down my neck. I wanted total privacy to work on my evil plan.

I went upstairs and shut my door firmly behind me. Mum was busy clearing out some kitchen cupboards, and she was pleased I hadn't just flopped down by the TV, so I guessed I was safe for a while.

I got out my art box. There was some card there, just perfect for my plan. I cut a bit to the right size and folded it in half. Then I smoothed it out again and on the front I drew a great big ghoulish heart with a few drops of blood dripping out of it. Then, so it wasn't too ghoulish, I drew a few flowers around the edge.

Then I got my gold felt tip pen and wrote in big romantic letters: *TO MY DARLING VALENTINE*. For the inside I got my black felt tip and disguised my handwriting. I wrote: *To sexy Yasmin. Your eyes are the colour of squirrel poo, your breath stinks of blue cheese, and you have the biggest*

*bum in Britain, but I've got the hots for you any-way. Meet me behind the boiler house at lunchtime and we can boil over together. All my love for ever, Dan.*

I had to smile as I wrote this sleazy message. There were four boys called Dan in our class and I imagined how puzzled Yasmin would be – and how insulted. She'd say to me, 'My God, Ruby, I can't think which one would be rude enough to send this!! Do you think it's Dan O'Hara? Or is the writing more like Dan Geoffreys?' And I'd just shrug and look puzzled.

I was going to slip it into her bag sometime tomorrow morning when she wasn't looking. It was going to be the greatest joke ever. I could hardly wait.

At supper Joe wasn't there. He must have gone round to Tiffany's. Mum had made a nice stew with baked potatoes, because of it being her day off, so there was plenty to eat for a change.

'It's nice without Tiffany,' I said. Mum sighed.

'She's not so bad, really, love,' she said. 'Just a bit immature.'

'Well, I hate her,' I said. Mum pulled a face. 'I hope she and Joe split up,' I went on. 'Because unless they do, let's face it, we're going to starve to death and she's going to end up obese.'

Dad smiled. Mum looked anxious.

'Well, they just might stay together,' said Mum. 'I remember how Grandpa disapproved of Dad when we were going out together.'

'Did he?' I asked, amazed. Grandpa Jones is the sweetest old guy in the world. I couldn't imagine him disapproving of anybody. Although he does shout at the TV when the golf's on.

'Well, my hair was a metre long in those days,' said Dad with a grin. 'And I only had a bath once a week. And I was in a rock band.'

'You were revolting,' said Mum. 'My parents were worried you'd end up on drugs or something.'

'Look at me now,' said Dad, patting his tummy. 'I'm a balding middle-aged geography teacher and the only thing I'm addicted to is your beef stew, sweetheart!'

'So there you are, Ruby,' said Mum. 'You never know, Joe and Tiffany might stay together and she might end up as your sister-in-law. And she might change a lot and turn out to be the nicest woman in the world.'

'Only with a complete personality transplant,' I growled.

## CHAPTER 9
# Oh no! This was big trouble!

N EXT DAY I arrived at school early
because Dad dropped me off on his way to
work. There weren't many people in the playground. I couldn't wait to see Yasmin and I'd
decided it would be best to be friendly as usual. I'd
been a bit distant with her for the past couple of
days, but now I had planned my glorious revenge,
it would be better to act totally normal. I didn't
want her suspecting me.

Lauren arrived and ran up, her funny awkward
legs sort of flailing out behind her as she ran.

'Hi, Ruby!' she gasped. 'Would you like to come and have tea with me tonight after school?' She looked eagerly into my face, standing a bit too close. I could smell tea on her breath. I didn't really want to accept the invitation. It was bad enough having to be with her all day. But what could I say? It would be cruel to refuse. I was the nearest thing to a friend she had at the moment, so I forced a grateful smile.

'Yes, I'd love to,' I said. 'I'll just text my mum and let her know.'

'And I'll text my mum to tell her it's OK!' grinned Lauren. There was a bit of bacon stuck between her front teeth. But she did look totally delighted. It was nice seeing her happy.

While we were doing our texting, Yasmin arrived, closely followed by Hannah. They seemed inseparable at the moment. Kind of practising for the pantomime horse, I guess.

'Hi, Rube. Hi, Lauren!' said Yasmin breezily. 'Only one day to go! Are your cossies ready?'

'Yes,' said Lauren, 'My mum finished my lion's mane last night. It's brilliant.'

'My mum's finished the pantomime horse,' said Hannah. 'Yasmin's coming round my house again tonight to try it on and practise.'

Yasmin gave me a quick little look, as if she felt guilty that she was spending so much time with Hannah and ignoring me.

'How's your costume coming along, Ruby?' she asked. 'What are you going as? A monkey?' I shrugged, but with a smile.

'I guess,' I said. 'I haven't decided yet. I'm always so last-minute.' I gave her a relaxed, friendly grin. I could afford to be – with my revenge tucked secretly away in my bag. Yasmin looked reassured. For a moment I felt fond of her again and wondered if this trick I was going to play on her was a bit mean, after all. Then she turned to Lauren.

'I'm gonna be sooo scared of you in your lion's outfit, Lauren!' she said with a mock shiver. 'We didn't think you'd come as a lion, did we, Hannah?'

Hannah giggled. 'No!' she said. 'We thought you'd come as a woolly mammoth!' And she burst into fits of giggles and ran off. Yasmin followed her. They galloped around the yard, whinnying like horses.

Lauren was blushing and looking down at the ground. You could see she was hurt and embarrassed, and I felt really cross that Yasmin and Hannah had been so mean. It was so obviously an insult – a comment on Lauren's appearance. The

big looming body, the woolly mass of hair . . .

'Ignore them, they're idiots sometimes,' I said, taking Lauren's arm. 'Tell me what the rest of your costume is like.'

Lauren started out on a long saga about a pair of stretchy pyjamas that was conveniently lion-coloured, and I tried to look interested, even though I was secretly keeping an eye open for Froggo. I still hadn't apologised to him for kicking his shin.

Lauren's arrival had caused so much hassle between me and my friends. It wasn't her fault, of course. She couldn't help being new and weird. I couldn't abandon her now. I couldn't bear it if she was hanging about by herself at lunchtime, looking big and sad and woolly.

The bell rang. We lined up in the yard and then walked in and took our coats off. It's always a bit of a scramble to get our coats off and hang them on the pegs, with people pushing past all the time. It's a bit like a rugby scrum, Mrs Jenkins says.

In an instant, I saw my chance. Yasmin's bag was right under my nose, and open. Yasmin had her back to me, doing up her shoelace. Loads of other people were around, but nobody was looking at me.

Quick as a flash, I whipped my spoof valentine card out of my bag and slipped it down inside hers, between two books. Then I turned and went

into the classroom. Lauren was already there. I sat down next to her, almost rubbing my hands with glee. I just couldn't wait to see Yasmin's face when she discovered the card in her bag.

I imagined how she'd be at break. She'd show me the card and say, 'Who can it be? Which Dan do you think it is? Do you think he really likes me?' She might even go up to one of the Dans and ask him if he'd sent it. And, oh boy, think of the reply she'd get! Those guys would certainly tell her where to go. I was giggling helplessly inside, though, of course, I kept a straight face because it was essential that whatever happened, Yasmin didn't suspect me.

We settled down, Mrs Jenkins took the register, and then she gave back the homework we'd done before – the diary of the chimney sweep. I got an A- for it. Mrs Jenkins had written: *Good work, Ruby. Imaginative!* I was pleased. I was a bit annoyed about the minus, though. Mrs Jenkins is quite harsh.

'Right, then,' she said, returning to her teacher's desk. 'Get out your copies of *The Jungle Book* Key Stage 2.'

I got mine out extra-fast so I could watch Yasmin fiddling in her bag. I saw the moment she caught sight of the mysterious envelope. I saw her look puzzled. She opened the envelope, still holding it half inside her bag, and took out the card. She read it. Her face went through a zillion expressions: shock, horror, embarrassment. She went bright red. I could hardly prevent myself from bursting out laughing.

But then she did something totally unexpected. Something totally off the script. Something she was so *not* meant to do. She got up and marched down to Mrs Jenkins' desk, carrying the card. She showed Mrs Jenkins the card and Mrs Jenkins inspected it carefully with a frown. A really scary frown.

76

My heart gave a panicky leap and started hammering away like mad. Oh no! This was big trouble! Mrs Jenkins told Yasmin to go back to her seat. Then, still holding the dreaded card, she looked around the class. She had a nasty, stern expression on her face. She looked especially hard and strict.

'Be quiet now, all of you, and listen to me!' she yelled in her frightening voice. Everybody was instantly still. You *so* don't want to get on the wrong side of Mrs Jenkins. 'Somebody's played a trick on Yasmin, and it's not funny!' snapped Mrs Jenkins. 'It's rude and it's nasty, and we're going to find out who's responsible, even if it takes all day!'

My heart turned to ice and my legs to jelly. It had all gone horribly wrong.

## CHAPTER 10
# Don't lie to me!

'RIGHT,' SAID Mrs Jenkins. 'Dan Collins, stand up!' Dan Collins looked surprised, and got to his feet. He's a tall boy with ginger hair.

'This looks like your work!' said Mrs Jenkins, waving the valentine crossly. 'You may think it's just a joke, but it's in very bad taste! What do you have to say for yourself?' Dan Collins blushed deeply, as if he was guilty or something.

'I didn't do it, miss!' he protested. 'I don't know anything about it!' His green eyes were huge and shocked. Mrs Jenkins glared at him for a moment – probably waiting for him to crack.

'Don't lie to me, Dan!' she snapped. Dan's eyes filled with tears. I felt dreadful.

'I'm not lying, miss!' he insisted, and his voice kind of broke slightly, as if he was trying not to cry.

'Hmmm . . .' Mrs Jenkins' face changed slightly. She still looked suspicious, but there were three other Dans in the room, and Dan Collins certainly looked as innocent as anyone has ever been. 'Sit down for a minute,' she said. Her gaze swivelled round the room. 'Dan O'Hara!' she barked.

Dan O'Hara struggled to his feet. He's quite a small boy with fluffy fair hair and pink cheeks. He always smells a bit of damp sheds, but I quite like him as he can do fantastic burps that go on for ages.

'Did you do this?' demanded Mrs Jenkins. Dan O'Hara looked bewildered and shook his head.

'No, miss,' he said. You could see his hands shaking slightly as he held on to the edge of the table. Mrs Jenkins glared at him. When she's angry her eyebrows become even more evil. She looked as if she could eat a whole barbecue, red hot coals and all, and not even need a glass of water afterwards. She looked as if she could eat Dan O'Hara.

'Dan Geoffreys!' she called in the voice of a mad, bad queen. 'Stand up!' Another Dan got up, looking totally amazed. This one was chubby with dark shiny black hair and an interest in crocodiles. But his love of reptiles couldn't save him now. 'What have you got to say about this?' demanded Mrs Jenkins. My heart was beating so fast, I thought everybody must be able to hear it. This was a nightmare. Any minute now, a Dan was going to be punished for something I had done.

'I don't know anything about it, miss!' said Dan Geoffreys, looking horrified. Mrs Jenkins was working herself up to a major strop. You could tell. Her cheeks were getting redder and redder, and her eyes were starting to flash. She glanced at the card once again, pulled a disgusted face and glared back at Dan Geoffreys. What on earth was going to happen next?

What happened was Hannah hiccuped. And at the back of the class, somebody sniggered. Mrs Jenkins' eyes kind of flared, so you could see the whites.

'Of course!' she snapped. 'Dan Skinner! Come down here!' I turned round to see Froggo getting out of his chair. He'd been the one who giggled. And now he was in big trouble. He walked down to the teacher's desk.

'I might have known it was you, Dan Skinner!' boomed Mrs Jenkins in her don't-mess-with-me voice. 'I think I recognise your handwriting! So you thought this was a big joke, did you?' She waved the card at him.

'No, miss!' insisted Froggo. 'I've never even seen it before!'

'I've had enough of this!' yelled Mrs Jenkins, her patience suddenly snapping. 'The whole lot of you can stay in at lunchtime and do extra work! All of the Dans!'

'But, miss . . .' protested Froggo. He was so brave.

I would never dare to challenge Mrs Jenkins, even with right on my side. 'That's not fair!'

'Don't you tell me what's fair!' shouted Mrs Jenkins. 'We've wasted enough time on this! Go back to your seat!'

Froggo went back. As he passed me he kind of secretly shrugged and opened his eyes really wide, as if to say, W*hat on earth's going on? What's this all about?*

'Right!' said Mrs Jenkins. 'Now everybody, let's see if we can manage to do some actual work for a change. Turn to page twenty-four . . .'

The rest of the lesson was a blur. I was in agony. I couldn't let all the Dans lose their lunch break just because I'd played a trick on Yasmin, and the trick had gone wrong. I had to own up. But how could I? Mrs Jenkins would be ten times crosser with me for just sitting there earlier and not saying a word while she interrogated all the Dans.

Finally, after what seemed like years of torture, but was probably only about half an hour, the bell rang. Everybody grabbed their bags and rushed out, because it was drama next with Mr Rivers. Adorable Mr Rivers, our favourite teacher.

Only I stayed behind. Mrs Jenkins was packing some papers away. I hung about miserably by her desk. I knew I had to admit it. Eventually she stopped fiddling with her bag, looked up and saw me.

'What is it, Ruby?' she snapped. She was so clearly irritated already, and she didn't even know of my dreadful crime — yet.

## CHAPTER 11
# My knees were shaking

'PLEASE, MISS,' I said, my heart beating in huge, slow throbs, 'I know who made the valentine.' Mrs Jenkins' eyes flared again. You could see she was interested.

'Who?' she snapped. I was now so scared, I could hardly speak. My knees were shaking.

'Me,' I croaked miserably. 'It was just a joke.'

Mrs Jenkins looked surprised, and then cross. 'Well, it's a pretty tasteless joke,' she said. 'I thought you and Yasmin were best friends?'

I hesitated. I didn't want to be a rat and say that

Yasmin hadn't bothered to look after Lauren at all. But on the other hand, it was true. I was surprised that Mrs Jenkins hadn't noticed. I opened my mouth ready to say something, but I was saved by Mrs Jenkins' mobile phone, which rang in her bag. She grabbed it and waved me off.

'Off you go!' she said crossly. 'You'll be late for drama. I'll deal with you later.'

I ran off. The thought of Mrs Jenkins dealing with me later was so awful, I couldn't enjoy drama at all, even when Mr Rivers asked us all to be seeds germinating in the earth and growing into trees. I wished I could change into a tree. Trees don't get into trouble, do they? Or get told off for playing tricks on people? Not as far as we know anyway.

Yasmin and Hannah were busy at break, practising their galloping. Lauren asked if she could read my fortune by looking at the lines on my hand. She said I was going to be a great success. I told her I was already a total failure, and she laughed. She thought it was a joke! After break we had maths and English. I normally love English but today I couldn't concentrate on anything. Mrs Jenkins kind of ignored me, but when the bell went for lunchtime, she said, 'The Dans needn't come to the classroom after all. The real author of the stupid card has been identified. See me at home time, Ruby.'

Everybody turned to look at me – some in amazement, some grinning, some shocked. I stared down at the table. There were patterns on it, swirling lines. You could tell it had been a tree, once. I wished I was lost in a magic forest. Anything but this: everybody staring at me and knowing I was going to be punished later.

Mrs Jenkins went out, but before anybody could say anything to me, I ran out to the playground on my own. I even left Lauren behind for once. I just wanted to be by myself. Besides, I was avoiding Yasmin, because now she knew it was me who'd made the valentine. I was also avoiding all the Dans, especially Froggo. I hadn't even managed to apologise to him yet for kicking him the other day. Let alone getting him into trouble this morning with my valentine, signed Dan.

I walked over to the railings and leaned against them, staring out into the road. A woman walked past with a toddler in a buggy. The toddler had a cute face with big blue eyes, and he smiled at me. I smiled back, but it was hard work. I'd never felt so depressed.

However was I going to face Yasmin and every-

body else, now they knew that it had been me? And worst of all, what punishment was Mrs Jenkins going to dish out later? I just hoped it had nothing to do with people looking at me. I hoped it would be a nice private punishment.

'Hey, Ruby!' I heard a cheerful voice. I looked up. Holly was walking along the pavement outside the school railings, holding hands with her weird Gothic boyfriend, Dom.

'Oh, hello, Holly,' I said.

'What's up, Ruby? You look fed up.'

'Oh, I'm just in trouble with Mrs Jenkins. She's

going to punish me later,' I said, shrugging. I didn't want to go into details. I didn't want Dom to know all my secret stuff.

'Never mind!' smiled Holly. 'If she's mean to you, just tell her I'll come round to her house and spit through the letterbox!' She and Dom laughed.

Just like last time, it was as if she was just using my problems as a way to amuse him. Usually Holly would have been sympathetic and a real help. This time she seemed to find it all hilarious. I said nothing, and kicked a stone about.

'Cheer up, Rube!' she went on. 'Think of all the lovely fun you'll have tomorrow at the fancy-dress party. I went round Zerrin's last night and Yasmin was telling us all about her pantomime horse. What are you going as? A monkey?'

'I suppose so,' I said. 'I haven't really organised it yet. I've got a brown jumper and a pair of brown tights. But I don't know about the face . . .' Suddenly I had an idea. 'Could you do me a monkey face make-up, Holly? Like you did before?' Holly bit her lip and looked thoughtful.

'I'm really sorry, Ruby, but we've got a band rehearsal after school for the gig. We're playing at the Valentine Ball. I sing with the band now, you know!'

'Don't worry, then,' I said gloomily. 'It's OK, fine.'

'Wait!' said Holly. 'I tell you what. I'm going home now with Dom to get a couple of CDs – I'll collect my face paints and I'll bring them here to you with a diagram of how to do the monkey face. Maybe Joe could do it for you? After all, he is an artistic genius!' She laughed again, and looked at Dom. He didn't laugh so much, this time. Maybe he was a bit wary of my talented bro. Maybe he thought Holly secretly fancied him or something.

'Oh, thanks,' I said. 'If I have the face paints and a diagram, I can probably do it myself.'

'OK,' said Holly. 'See you at 3.30!' And she strolled off arm-in-arm with Dom.

I was just beginning to feel a bit better — but only a bit — when suddenly somebody grabbed my hair from behind, and pulled really, really hard. I whirled round, but they didn't let go. All the roots of my hair kind of shrieked in agony. It was Yasmin, and Froggo was running up as well. Oh, no! It seemed as if I was about to be beaten up — by my best friends!

## CHAPTER 12
# That was a horrible thing to do

YASMIN WAS pulling my hair. Her face loomed up at me, furious and kind of twisted.

'You pig, Ruby!' she hissed. 'You cow! How could you play such an evil trick? I hate you!'

I screamed. I know I'm supposed to be cool, but it's hard not to scream when your hair is being pulled out – especially by your best friend.

'Go for it, Yas!' yelled Froggo. 'Kill the beast!' And he kicked me.

'Oh, don't!' shouted somebody nearby. 'Stop it! Don't fight!' I think it was Lauren.

Yasmin screwed up her fist really hard, so every hair on my head seemed to shriek in protest. Then she wheeled me round. I staggered about, helpless. I wished I'd never made that stupid card. It was only supposed to be a joke.

'Stop that!' came a sudden grown-up voice. 'Yasmin, let go!' It was Mrs Parker, one of the teaching assistants. She patrols the playground at lunchtime to make sure we don't kill each other. She's like a sort of cop. And boy, was I glad to see her.

Yasmin let go of my hair and I stood up, massaging my scalp. My head was still smarting. Mrs Parker is a chubby woman with red curly hair and

thick glasses. She looked at me. Her eyes seemed huge.

'Are you OK, Ruby?' she asked. I nodded. 'What's this all about?' she demanded, looking round at all of us. I was silent. Yasmin was silent, Froggo was silent. We all just stared at the ground. 'Oh all right, then,' sighed Mrs Parker. 'Just don't let me see any more of that kind of behaviour. OK? Yasmin?' Yasmin looked up and nodded. 'Off you go, then,' said Mrs Parker. 'Don't waste your precious playtime arguing and fighting.'

We ran off – in opposite directions, obviously. I went to the furthest corner, where there's a kind of overhanging tree from the garden of the house next door. I stood there, right in the corner, under the tree. Although it was winter, it still has its leaves, and I was grateful. It made a private little corner.

'Ruby?' came a voice. Oh, what now? I turned around. It was Lauren. 'Are you OK, Ruby?' I nodded. Lauren looked kind of awkward and shy – even more than usual. 'Would you like my chocolate milkshake? I don't want it.' Lauren held the bottle out to me.

'Thanks,' I said. I took it, and gulped down several mouthfuls.

'Finish it,' said Lauren. 'I don't want any.' So I did. It tasted nice. Then I handed the empty bottle back to her.

'Thanks,' I said. 'Wait. Let's put it in the recycling bin.' I took the bottle back from her. Everything was always so awkward with Lauren. I set off towards the recycling corner where the bins are for the glass and plastic and stuff. Lauren tagged along.

'Never mind,' said Lauren, trying to comfort me. 'We'll give you a lovely tea tonight. Do you like cheese scones?' Oh no! I'd completely forgotten that I'd promised to go to Lauren's for tea tonight! What a disaster!

'Yes,' I said, but I didn't sound keen. I sounded as if she'd promised me a delicious stone, covered in slime and newt poo.

I was having such a rubbish day, I just wanted to go home. And the torment hadn't finished yet, either. Mrs Jenkins was going to punish me at the end of school. Oh yes! There was that horror still to come.

The only real thing to look forward to was seeing Holly. If she lent me her face paints and a diagram, I could at least get my monkey outfit right for the party tomorrow.

All through afternoon school I was dreading the punishment that Mrs Jenkins was going to dish out. When the bell went for home time, everyone else ran out to get their coats, but I stayed behind.

'Ruby?' said Mrs Jenkins. She seemed to be thinking of something else. 'Oh yes, Ruby. That stupid valentine. That was a horrible thing to do.'

'Sorry,' I said. 'It was meant to be a joke.'

'It was in very bad taste,' said Mrs Jenkins. But as she spoke, she was packing her bag. That meant she didn't think my crime was so very awful. If I

was in serious trouble she'd be standing there with her arms folded, looking fierce.

'Now listen to me,' said Mrs Jenkins, straightening up and staring down into my face. 'You and Yasmin have always been best friends, haven't you?'

'Yes,' I said. It came out as a kind of croak.

'Well, then, I don't have to tell you that Yasmin's a lovely girl. She's bright, in fact, she's highly intelligent. She's beautiful, she's confident, she's a go-getter. Right?'

'Yes,' I nodded. It was true that Yasmin was all those things. But I was starting to feel jealous. Yasmin was also a bit ruthless and sometimes she got carried away by crazy ideas. And she hadn't helped me look after Lauren, at all. But there was no point in saying so.

'You're an imaginative girl,' said Mrs Jenkins. 'You're talented.' Hmm, this was getting better. But she still hadn't said I was beautiful and highly intelligent like blinking blasted blessed blithering Yasmin. 'Put your talents to use in a positive way,' Mrs Jenkins went on. 'Not by hurting people's feelings. OK, Ruby?'

'Yes,' I said. I was annoyed that she hadn't said I was beautiful and highly intelligent like Yasmin. But at least she hadn't mentioned actual punishment yet. I liked Mrs Jenkins' tone of voice. She sounded almost friendly.

'I'm sorry,' I said, and hung my head. It's always best in these situations to be as meek and apologetic as you can. I'd *crawl* to avoid getting told off. I'd eat dirt.

'Run along, now,' said Mrs Jenkins with a sigh, as if she was tired of me and my problems. I exited at speed.

I was beginning to feel a tiny bit better. No punishment from Jenko! Just a pep-talk! I was amazed. I dived into my coat. Things were really looking up. And Holly would be waiting at the school gate with the face paints. I grabbed my bag and ran out.

But Holly wasn't waiting at the gate. Instead Lauren was there, with her surprisingly small mum. Oh heck! I was going to have to go off to their house and I'd miss Holly! I could hardly say, *Sorry, but could we hang about here until my friend Holly comes with the face paints?*

Why did Holly have to be late? She was usually so reliable. I was sure it had something to do with that Dom. He's a bad influence.

As I reached the gate, Mrs Potter smiled at me and Lauren looked pleased and kind of proud that I was going home with her. Luckily, most people had gone home already so none of my friends could see me going off home with the nerdy new girl. It was obviously going to be the nerdiest tea ever. With nerd sandwiches and nerd-flavoured yogurt, possibly.

I wondered how soon I'd be able to get away. Maybe I should pretend to feel sick. Then they'd have to take me home early. Maybe I should pretend to feel sick right now. Then they'd go off without me and I could wait here for Holly.

'Hi, Ruby!' said Lauren's mum with a happy smile.

'Hi!' I replied. She looked so really happy, I didn't have the heart to say I felt sick.

'Lauren's thrilled you're coming to tea!' trilled Mrs P. Lauren looked annoyed at her mum. Obviously, that *thrilled* was a mistake. It made Lauren sound needy and mad. Like my stalker or something. So Lauren was irritated by her mum. This was going to be the teatime from hell.

As I got into their car, my mobile rang. It was a text from Holly. *SORRY I CAN'T MAKE IT RUBY BABE – GOT HELD UP. LOVE, HOL X.*

This was typical of the whole day so far. My revenge valentine had misfired, landing me in

deep embarrassing trouble. I'd been attacked by
my best friend, told off by my teacher, abandoned
by my former idol, and now I was speeding to
some kind of terrible tea where, possibly, I would
be offered nourishing snake sandwiches and a
refreshing glass of dragon's pee.

## CHAPTER 13
# What are you wishing for?

**W**E DROVE right out of town. The houses gave way to trees and hills. I like that sort of thing. If only our country had monkeys in the trees. But I could only see sheep. Mrs Potter was chattering away to Lauren about something to do with their dog, who'd had a thorn in its paw or something. I sat in silence, trying not to look moody.

We turned off the main road down a muddy lane. Hedges scraped the side of the car. This was quite exciting.

'Those are our sheep,' said Lauren. The sheep were everywhere. There was a hill up ahead, and they were just all over it.

'What, all of them?' I asked, amazed.

'Yes,' laughed Lauren. 'You can come and see the lambs.'

We rounded a bend in the lane and there was a big old farmhouse, surrounded by interesting barns and sheds. We drew up in the yard and Lauren jumped out. Her face was kind of lit up: relaxed and happy. She looked totally different from the awkward new girl at school.

'Maybe Ruby would like a ride on Charlie before it gets dark,' said Lauren's mum. 'You can go in the lambing shed later.'

'Great!' said Lauren. 'Would you like a ride on the pony, Ruby?'

'Wow!' I was really excited. 'I'd love one! But I've never ridden before.'

'Don't worry,' said Lauren cheerfully. 'Charlie's really quiet. I'll walk along with you. It'll be fine. Come on!'

Lauren fixed me up with all the right gear: the boots, the hat, everything. Then we went into the stable. Charlie was the cutest pony you could imagine. He was grey, with long white eyelashes and big, cute, dark grey, slobbery lips.

'Hello, darling!' said Lauren, patting his cheek and giving him a sugar lump. 'This is Ruby. Ruby, this is Charlie.'

'Hi, Charlie!' I said rather shyly, as I am not a horsy sort of person and had never been introduced to one before.

'Stroke his cheeks!' said Lauren, while Mrs Potter was fixing the saddle. 'Breathe into his nostrils.'

I stroked his cheeks. His hair was tough, like the hair on a coconut, and it smelt nice. I breathed shyly into his nostrils. This was better than dating boys. I should imagine so, anyway. Lauren led Charlie out into the yard.

'OK,' said Lauren. 'Put that foot into the stirrup, and hold on to the saddle with that hand. Then swing yourself up.' I did as she said, and suddenly I was sitting on Charlie's back! It was amazing.

'There you are!' beamed Lauren. 'Easy, wasn't it?' Lauren was now suddenly some kind of wonderful expert. Before she had just been a sad nerd. How things can change.

Lauren showed me how to sit with my feet in the stirrups, and she held the bridle and walked Charlie round the yard. Mrs Potter went back indoors to make the tea.

'OK,' said Lauren. 'We'll just go on a little walk down Briars Lane.' She led Charlie out and soon we were going down a lovely lane. I could see over the hedges. The sun came out. It was pretty near perfect.

'Poor old Yasmin!' I said. 'She's only got a pantomime horse – and here I am riding the real thing!' I was so excited, my face was sort of grinning all by itself. Lauren smiled up at me.

'Charlie's lovely, isn't he?' she said. 'He's so quiet, even Roly can ride on him, and he's only four.'

After our ride we put Charlie back in his stable and I gave him a cuddle. I so loved that pony.

'You can come over and ride him any time you like!' said Lauren. Her cheeks were pink and flushed and her eyes sparkled. She didn't look shadowy and awkward at all. She was now almost beautiful! How bizarre. It was almost like some kind of magic spell.

Inside the farm kitchen there was the most scrumptious smell of something baking with cheese. Three little kids were running about, and you know how it is, it seemed like three hundred.

'Alfie!' called Lauren as we entered. 'Alice! Roly! Come and meet my friend Ruby!' They came rushing up.

'Hi, Ruby,' said Alfie. He had divine curls and was about eight years old.

'Hello, Ruby,' said Alice. She had no front teeth and looked like a pretty little vampire. 'I'm thix.' I assumed this was her way of saying *six*.

'Harrow, Wooby!' said the littlest one, a boy with round cheeks like a baby. He spoke without taking his thumb out of his mouth. It was the cutest thing that had happened in my life for some time.

'Hello, Alfie,' I said. 'Hello, Alice! Hello . . .'

'Woly,' said Roly.

'Here you are, Ruby,' said Lauren. 'You can have the special chair.' The chair was a lovely old carved chair with a tapestry seat.

'Great-grandma made that seat,' said Mrs Potter. 'We always call it the special chair. The first time you sit in it, you make a wish.'

I didn't quite know what to wish for. Everybody was quiet, watching.

'What are you wishing for?' asked Alfie. 'Is it a car?'

'Don't athk, Alfie!' said Alice. 'It'th thuppothed to be a thecret.'

I racked my brains. I couldn't think what to wish for. I was so tempted to wish that Joe would split up with Tiffany. Or Holly split up with Dom. But it seemed kind of mean to waste my wish on something so harsh. I closed my eyes.

*I wish . . .* I thought, *that Lauren will be happy at school, and loads of other people will realise how nice she is.* It seemed a more polite sort of wish to make. After all, I was sitting in her great-grandma's chair. I opened my eyes. They were all smiling at me.

Then the tea began. Tea? It was a feast. The cheese scones were fresh from the oven, warm and scrumptious. Then there was bread and butter.

'Home-made bread,' said Mrs Potter. 'And home-made jam.' It tasted fantastic.

'And home-made chocolate cake,' said Lauren. We pigged out until we were almost bursting.

'Wow!' I gasped, when I'd finished. 'That was the best tea ever. Thanks a lot, Mrs Potter.' Lauren's mum smiled and said it was a pleasure. 'It's a good job I rode Charlie before I had my tea, or I'd have broken his back!' I laughed.

Roly got down from his chair, came around the table to where I was and put his arms round me.

'I yike Wooby,' he said. Then he climbed up on

to my knee and cuddled me. It was the nicest feeling. It may sound strange, but I'd never been cuddled by a little kid before. None of my other friends have got really small bros and sisters. Roly's head snuggled against my chest. His hair smelt lovely. I gave him a hug. He was so heavy, I got pins and needles in my legs. But I didn't care.

Lauren, Alfie and Alice helped their mum clear away the dishes while I just sat and snuggled up with Roly. It was love at first sight. I couldn't have loved him more – unless he'd been a monkey.

'OK, Ruby,' said Lauren. 'What would you like to see first? The piglets or the lambs?'

'The piglets, please,' I said. We put our coats on and went out into the yard. By now it was getting dark, so Lauren carried a torch. The barns were lit up, though. The light coming out of the barn doors was the colour of orange juice. It looked cosy and Christmassy.

We went into a door that was sort of cut in half – a stable door, I think they're called. Inside, fast asleep in a great pile of straw, was a huge mother pig with about ten tiny piglets. She was lying on her side and snoring. All the little ones were lying beside her in a row.

When they heard us, they got up and trotted over to investigate. They grunted in their deep voices. They nibbled and sniffed at our shoes with their little snouts.

'You can stroke them,' said Lauren. 'But don't lift them up, or they'll squeal, and their mum will be cross.'

I bent down and touched a piglet. Its back felt tough and strong and there were stiff little white hairs all over its skin.

'That one's called Princess,' said Lauren. 'Scratch her side – she likes that.'

I scratched Princess's side and she rolled over, grunting gently. I touched her snout. It felt strong and rubbery. This was the best time I'd had since riding the pony.

After a long time petting the piglets, Lauren suggested I might like to go into the lambing shed. It was a big barn, divided up into little pens where mother sheep looked after their baby lambs. Some had twins, some had triplets, some had just one.

'This is my favourite,' said Lauren. 'I call her Lucinda.' She leaned over the side of the pen and scooped up the tiniest and fluffiest little lamb in the world. The top of its head was covered with thick woolly curls. Lauren kissed Lucinda's curls and then passed her over to me.

It was like having a living teddy bear. I cuddled her and sniffed at her wool. It smelt lovely – clean and soft and sheepy. Her delicate little hooves were black, like high-heeled shoes. She bleated softly.

'I've fallen in love!' I grinned. 'For the third time since I came here – no, the fourth, I fell in love with Roly too. Charlie, Roly, Priscilla and Lucinda.'

Lauren looked pleased. 'Good,' she said. 'You've had a good time, then?'

'A good time?' I laughed. 'I'm in heaven.'

In the end, though, it was time to go home. I kissed everyone goodbye and promised to come again soon. On the way home, I thought how ironical it was. I'd been planning to say I was sick so I could go home early. Or even not come at all. Now I was going home really, really late and it still seemed too soon.

'Did you have a nice time at Lauren's, love?' asked Mum, as I burst into the kitchen.

'The best!' I grinned. 'They've got piglets, lambs and I even rode on the pony!'

'Oh, how lovely!' said Mum. 'So this is quite a good day for you, then, isn't it? And this is for you, too.' She pointed to a big cardboard box lying on the floor.

'What is it?' I asked. For a moment I wondered if Yasmin had brought a present round as a peace offering.

'Open it and see,' said Mum. I took off the lid and pulled off the wrapping paper. What I saw really made me jump. It was a gorilla's face looking up at me!

'It's a baby gorilla suit,' said Mum. 'For the fancy-dress party tomorrow.'

I was amazed. I pulled it out and held it up. The furry body, the black gorilla hands – and the head, which you pulled on separately like a balaclava. I dived into the head straight away. I could see through the holes for the eyes. Mum looked amused.

'It's wonderful!' she said. 'It's ever so realistic!' I pulled the head off again, and grabbed the suit.

'I'm going to change into the whole thing!' I yelled, crazy with joy. 'How lovely of Holly to lend me it!'

'It wasn't Holly!' said Mum, looking mysterious.

'Who was it, then? Was it you, Mum? Thanks so much!' I hugged her.

'No,' said Mum with a weird smile. 'It wasn't me. It was Tiffany.'

Suddenly everything seemed topsy-turvy. The world seemed upside down. My life seemed inside out and back to front.

My best mate Yasmin had attacked me, and then nerdy Lauren had given me the best time ever. My idol Holly had let me down, and now horrid Tiffany had got this amazing gorilla suit for me.

But I didn't waste much time thinking about how odd it all was. I had an important job to do – transforming myself into one of the great apes. It was going to be the most fantastic moment of my entire life.

## CHAPTER 14

# Who is it? Who is it?

I RAN UPSTAIRS and locked myself in the bathroom and dived into my gorilla suit. It was perfect. I looked at myself in the mirror and actually squealed in delight. A real, live baby gorilla stood there! I swung my arms about and I scratched myself in an ape-like way. It was amazing, truly amazing.

Tiffany had gone home because it was quite late, but when I saw her again I'd have to give her an extra-special thank you. Perhaps even a kiss. I couldn't believe how wonderful this gorilla suit was. I wanted to wear it *all night*.

But first I ran downstairs and bounded into the TV room, where Dad and Joe were watching some football. I made gorilla noises and beat my chest. They laughed. Then I ambled into the kitchen, where Mum was sitting doing a crossword, and I grabbed a banana with my black gorilla hands. She laughed and screamed and everything.

'Ooooh, it's ever so realistic!' she said. 'Tiffany got it from the dress hire place – isn't she clever?'

'Oh-oh-oh-oh-oh!' I replied in apespeak. So far I had hated Tiffany. But now I felt I really should start again with her. When I saw her next I'd be really nice. It was so kind of her to get me that out-fit. Even if she was secretly trying to impress Joe. I didn't mind.

I swung upstairs, climbed my ladder and entered the tree house. 'Get outta here!' yelled Stinker in alarm. 'Who the blazes are you?' shouted Hewitt. Funky fainted. Then I took my gorilla head off and they could see it was me.

'Phew!' said Stinker. 'You had me worried there, for a moment. I thought some big shot was movin' in on our territory.'

Mum said I couldn't sleep in my gorilla suit,

which was slightly irritating, but otherwise I fell asleep in the best mood ever.

Next day we packed the gorilla suit into its cardboard box to take it to school. Everybody had boxes or bags with their costumes in, and we stashed them safely in Mrs Jenkins' cupboard.

Yasmin didn't speak to me. She didn't even look at me. She sat at the other side of the room with Hannah, and they did a lot of giggling. I ignored her. Lauren sat beside me as usual and she told me that Alice, Roly and Alfie had begged her to bring me home for tea again today.

'They adore you!' she said. I felt odd. It was love-ly being adored. I had never thought it would ever happen to me. 'You've got a fan club, Ruby!' grinned Lauren.

The whole day was slightly odd because of being St Valentine's. Some people had cards and they showed them around: there was a lot of teasing and mystery and kind of soppy jokes. But I was focussed on the party after school. I hadn't told anybody about my costume, not even Lauren. I couldn't wait to transform myself into an ape again.

Finally the bell went for end of school. We all collected our boxes and bags and went off to the cloakroom to change. I took my box into the girls' loos. I didn't want anybody to see me till the transformation was complete.

I ripped off my school clothes and jumped into my gorilla suit. I pulled on the head. Then I burst out of the cubicle and bounded out into the school hall, where everybody was gathering. There was a gigantic scream as I appeared!

I ran around the room, lurching from side to side like apes do, and occasionally resting my weight on my knuckles. I beat my chest. I did an ape call. Everybody was staring at me in amazement and laughing. Some people were even clapping and cheering.

'Who is it? Who is it?' I heard them all saying. I
ran up to the pantomime horse and pretended to
groom it. I pretended to find a little flea on its
back and I ate it. Everybody shrieked in disgust
and got hysterical giggles. Then I ran off and
jumped up on to the platform. I was so excited, I
hardly knew what I was doing. Then I heard a big
shout:

'STOP that monkey business! Quiet everybody!'

It was lovely Mr Rivers. I stood still and stared
down at him. I hoped he wasn't angry. I hoped I
hadn't gone too far. But Mr Rivers had a smile on
his face.

'OK, Kid Kong, calm down,' he said. Everybody laughed. Kid Kong! That was a good one. 'It's like a zoo in here!' said Mr Rivers. Everybody laughed again. 'But listen, folks, we have to keep the noise down. There's loads of games to play and we won't be able to do that unless we cooperate. OK? So come down off there, Kid Kong, and will everybody sit down on the floor, for a start – except the pantomime horse. You can remain standing.'

I joined the others on the floor. Lauren, in her lion's outfit, was talking to a cat. It was nice to see her making friends. Maybe my wish had come true. Froggo came and sat next to me. He was dressed like a dinosaur: T Rex. It was a good costume. His dinosaur head was above his face, sort of like a professional cyclist's helmet. His own face looked out from between its teeth. He tried to peep into my head through the eye-holes.

'Who are you?' he asked. 'Are you Ruby? It's an amazing costume.'

'Oh-oh-oh-oh-oh!' I answered, nodding. Froggo grinned.

'Amazing!' he said. 'I'm so jealous, I'm almost tempted to go extinct.'

It was great being mates with Froggo again. He didn't apologise for kicking me. I didn't apologise for kicking him. We seemed to be calling it quits.

We played loads of games. Even normal games such as Musical Chairs seemed a lot more fun with us all dressed as animals. The pantomime horse bumped and barged about. Its back end kept falling over and it looked really funny.

'OK!' said Mrs Jenkins, smiling (even she was in party mood – maybe, who knows, she had got a valentine?) 'Now we're all going to have our tea.'

We went back to our classrooms for the tea. At this point, obviously, I had to take my head off. The air felt cool and everybody grinned at me and told me how great my outfit was.

The pantomime horse was unzipped, and Hannah and Yasmin climbed out. Yasmin was very red in the face, and her hair was so sweaty it was plastered all over her brow. She didn't look very happy, to be honest. She came over and sat down with me and Lauren and Froggo.

'Hi, Ruby!' she said. 'Your costume is amazing!' She gave me a kind of slightly nervous smile. She clearly wanted to be friends again.

'Your costume is amazing, too,' I said. Yasmin pulled a face and shook her head.

'It's awful,' she said. 'I hate it. It's so hot in there. I can't see where I'm going. I keep falling over and hurting myself. And all the time Hannah's bum is in my face. Some party! It's the worst mistake I've ever made in my life!'

'Cheer up!' said Lauren. 'Have a crisp.' And she held out the plate politely.

'Thanks, Lauren,' said Yasmin, taking one. We all sat and guzzled happily, though Yasmin still looked quite grumpy. And of course, because she'd had to get out of the pantomime horse, she didn't have a costume on. Just her school clothes, looking all crumpled.

'I had a ride on a real horse yesterday,' I said. 'At Lauren's.'

Yasmin's eyes went kind of huge and her face suddenly changed colour – turned sort of green, with envy, I suppose. She stared at Lauren in an entirely new way: with respect.

'You've got a horse?' she gasped.

'Well, a pony,' said Lauren with a modest shrug. 'You can come and ride him too, one day, if you like.'

Although I was pleased that Yasmin and Lauren seemed to be making friends at last, I did kind of secretly hope that Alfie, Alice and Roly wouldn't adore her quite as much as they adored me.

After a while, Lauren went off to the loo. Yasmin leaned close to me and whispered, 'I was wrong about Lauren. You were right, Rube. She's amazing! I'm going to make friends with her right now! I gotta have a ride on that pony!'

'She's also got piglets, lambs, and cows and stuff,' I told her. Yasmin's eyes grew large again.

'Wow! You're so lucky, Ruby! Listen – I'm sorry I was mean recently. Let's be friends again. We can have a threesome with Lauren and ride her pony on a daily basis for the rest of our lives. OK?'

I gave Yas a hug. It was good to be friends again. She can be really funny. And when she's been wrong and horrid, she always admits it.

When Lauren came back, she started talking to Yasmin all about her farm. This left me free to chat with Froggo.

'I was going to send you a valentine, just for a laugh,' said Froggo, 'but I decided it would be too disgusting and soppy.' He finished his lemonade and burped loudly.

'I was going to send you one too,' I said. 'But I decided it would be lame and gross.'

'We were so right not to,' said Froggo. 'Let's make a bargain that we'll never send each other valentines as long as we live.'

We shook hands to seal the bargain and grinned. It was so much better, so much more fun having a no-valentines bargain than going through all that lame giggling and teasing stuff over soppy cards. Ugh!

When the party ended, Mum came to pick me up. I had had to change back into my school clothes (which I'd left in the girls' toilets, on the floor – thank goodness Mrs Jenkins didn't notice.)

'Is Tiffany at home?' I asked. 'I want to thank her for getting the gorilla costume for me.'

'Er – she rang to ask if we'd mind taking the costume back to the dress hire place,' said Mum. 'Apparently she and Joe have split up again.'

'Oh no!' I said. 'I was just starting to like her.'

'They'll probably be back together again by next weekend,' said Mum. 'I think she was hurt because he didn't send her a valentine. And that led to a little row.'

When we got home, Joe was up in his room, playing very loud rap music. This is always a sign that he's feeling cross. I wondered if he and Tiffany were finished for good. Though I was very grateful to Tiffany for finding the gorilla suit for me, I still wanted Joe to go out with Holly, not Tiffany.

First, though, I'd have to crack the problem of Holly being with Dom. That would have to be my next project. I wasn't looking forward to being a teenager with all that dating rubbish. It really seemed to mess up your life.

I put on my gorilla suit one more time and went up into my tree house to chill out with my monkeys.

WANT TO JOIN RUBY'S GANG?

Look out for the Ruby Rogers Club
and receive Ruby updates and goodies!

Go to
www.suelimbbooks.co.uk/Ruby
to join the club and turn the page for a sneak
preview of Ruby's next brilliant caper . . .

# RUBY ROGERS

Result!

Hannah has two dogs. Yasmin has a cat. And Lauren has cows and sheep and pigs and dogs *and* a cat! And a pony!'

'Yes, but Lauren lives on a farm, love,' said Mum. Her soft Welsh voice was beginning to sound a bit edgy.

'I agree,' said Joe with a mocking look on his face. 'It's not fair. I want a cow and I want it now. With mustard, ketchup and chips.' He did an evil grin at his own stupid joke.

'Look,' said Mum, 'You know Lauren's family are ever so fond of you. Her little brothers and sisters adore you. They said you'd be welcome to go there any time. Why don't you ask if you can go this weekend? There are still baby lambs being born every day, I expect. That would be nice, wouldn't it, love?'

'I don't want to have to go to Lauren's every time I want to cuddle an animal!' I snapped. 'I want to have one right here in our house. I want a pet. Everybody else has a pet! It's *so* not fair!'

Read on for a taster of what's to come in . .

# Ruby Rogers
# Result!

'IT'S SO NOT FAIR!' I was furious. 'It's completely and utterly totally mean and horrid!' I clenched my fists. I clenched my fists. I clenched my fists till they hurt. Everybody else at the table stopped eating. Mum looked surprised and cross. Dad looked nervous. Joe started to cook up a nasty smile. He loves it when I'm in a rage.

'Listen, Ruby, sweetheart,' said Mum, putting down her knife and fork, 'We explained a while ago that –'

'But it's not FAIR!' I yelled. 'I know what you're going to say but it's not FAIR!!! Dan has a dog.